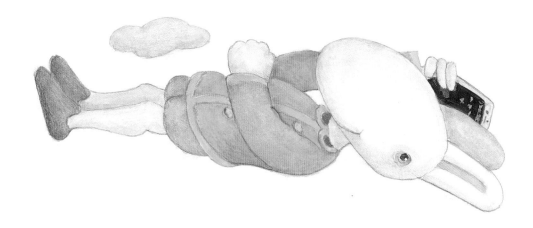

DOWN & UP

Etienne Delessert

Creative Editions

Up to no good...

What's up?

Fired up!

Spruced up!

Lit up!

Wrapped
up...

Back down.

Text and illustrations copyright © 2021 by Etienne Delessert   Edited by Kate Riggs   Designed by Rita Marshall
Published in 2021 by Creative Editions   P. O. Box 227, Mankato, MN 56002 USA
Creative Editions is an imprint of The Creative Company   www.thecreativecompany.us
Library of Congress Cataloging-in-Publication Data   Names: Delessert, Etienne, author, illustrator.
Title: Up & down / by Etienne Delessert. Summary: Familiar phrases and unusual characters accompany
a boy as he ascends and descends in an elevator. Identifiers: LCCN 2020053401 / ISBN 978-1-56846-380-3
Subjects: CYAC: Imagination–Fiction. / Elevators–Fiction. Classification: LCC PZ7.D3832 Up 2021   DDC [E]–dc23
First edition 9 8 7 6 5 4 3 2 1